GYPSY'S CLEANING DAY

Ellen Eagle

Morrow Junior Books New York

Printed in Hong Kong by South China Printing Company (1988) Ltd.
1   2   3   4   5   6   7   8   9   10
Library of Congress Cataloging-in-Publication Data
Eagle, Ellen.
Gypsy's cleaning day/Ellen Eagle.
p.   cm.
Summary: A food-obsessed golden retriever with too many
possessions generously shares them with a needy friend—and manages
to clean her house at the same time.
ISBN 0-688-07391-3.—ISBN 0-688-07392-1 (lib. bdg.)
[1. Dogs—Fiction. 2. Pigs—Fiction. 3. Friendship—Fiction.]
I. Title.
PZ7.E116Gy   1990
[E]—dc20   89-34315   CIP   AC

FOR GORDON,
this would be my gift to you
except that you gave it to me first
and
FOR ZACHARY,
now Gypsy can stay with you
always

"Where is my paisley scarf?" Gypsy wondered.

She had looked everywhere, and this is what she'd found:

her pink-and-yellow
baba blanket,

a Godzilla pull toy,
her windup car,
a squeaky chicken leg,

and a tuna fish
sandwich.

But there was no paisley scarf.

Gypsy looked in the mirror. "I have too many things," she told her reflection. "Today will be my cleaning day."

Gypsy began by eating the tuna fish sandwich. Just then there was a knock at the door.

"Number 18 Goldenhair Lane?" asked the police officer on Gypsy's front porch. "Report of a robbery, Ma'am?" He looked past Gypsy into her home. "What a MESS!" he gasped. "Don't you worry, Ma'am. We'll catch the lowlife that did this to you."

"There wasn't any lowlife," Gypsy told him. "And this is Number 17 Goldenhair Lane. Number 18 is Pig's house, over there."

They looked across the lane. Pig was running back and forth on her front lawn.

A robbery at Pig's house! Gypsy was aghast. "Today is my cleaning day," she said softly, "but friendship comes first."

Gypsy and the police officer crossed over to Pig's house. Pig didn't even give them time to speak. "It's . . . it's Cousin Parfel," she cried. "He's struck again!" Pig was turning from pink to red. She waved a piece of paper in front of them. But it wasn't a piece of paper. It was a photograph. It was Parfel!

"Oh, Pig!" Gypsy said. The police officer looked confused.

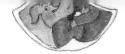

"I heard that Parfel was in town. I padlocked the door when I left this morning, but a window must have been open. He left me this photograph!" Pig wasn't crying anymore. She was yelling.

"My family treasures — all gone." Pig led Gypsy and the police officer into the house.

Gypsy blinked in surprise at the almost empty room.

Pig wailed, "My purple rug with 'To Pig from Mommy' embroidered on it, gone! My little pink piano, gone!"

The police officer took out a pad and pencil. "Where are they gone *to,* Ma'am?" he asked.

"Halfway around the world to Bora Bora, that's where!" Pig shouted.
"To Bora Bora with Cousin Parfel!"

The officer began to write.

"B-O-R-A B-O-R-A," Pig spelled. "That's where Parfel lives when he isn't here breaking into my house."

Our Vermont Vacation

Such a fine, graceful lamp

Hanging Around at Home

Our Florida Vacation

I travel the world with my china

Together in Paris

From Momm

August in Alsace

"Just look! My rocking chair and my patchwork quilt—both on Bora Bora! My pelican lamp, on Bora Bora! He always claimed that Grandma meant to give her treasures to him, not to me—that it was all a horrible mistake. And he's been after my things ever since. But I'll get them back. I'll get them all back!"

"We're on the case, Ma'am," promised the police officer as he left.
"Some help he was." Pig sniffed. "What hurts the most," she said sadly
to Gypsy, "is the thought of my hand-painted china teacups on Bora Bora."
There was one chair left in the room. Pig sat on it.

"Pig, you look weak," Gypsy said. "What you need is food. Come to my
house for lunch. It was my cleaning day, but a friend in need comes first."
They closed Pig's door and walked slowly across the lane.

Pig peered through Gypsy's doorway. "How can we have lunch in the middle of all that?" Pig asked. "There's no place to sit."

Gypsy had to admit that Pig was right. She sniffed the cool, fresh air. "It's such a beautiful day," she said. "We'll have lunch right here on the porch! I'll be just a minute."

Pig sat down heavily. "Some beautiful day," she grumbled. "I'll bet it's a beautiful day on Bora Bora."

Gypsy was gone for a long time. Pig's stomach was growling when she finally came back.

"I thought we'd have spaghetti with tomato sauce, Pig," she said.
"I love spaghetti with tomato sauce!"
"But I couldn't find the spaghetti or the tomato sauce."
"Oh."

"So I thought we'd have ice-cream sandwiches."
"I love ice-cream sandwiches. All flavors!"
"But I finished the ice cream for breakfast."
"Oh."

"Then I thought we'd have graham crackers with marshmallows and melted chocolate."

"That's my favorite . . ." Pig began enthusiastically.

"But I couldn't find any, Pig," Gypsy told her. "And I couldn't find the frozen hot-dog pizza, either."

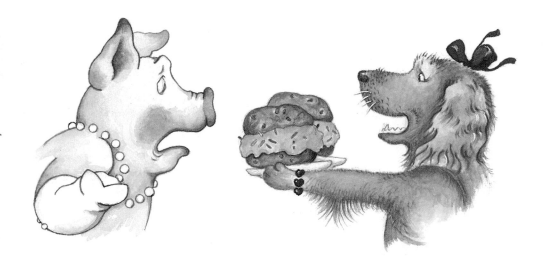

Pig felt worse than ever. "So what are we having for lunch?" she asked.

"Peanut butter," Gypsy said happily, "with candy sprinkles on a cinnamon-raisin bagel!"

Gypsy took a big bite out of her bagel. "Say, Pig, did I ever tell you my dream about the cheddar cheeseburger?"

"Yes," Pig grumbled. "At least forty times."

"It was a big cheeseburger. It was so big I needed a bicycle to get from one end to the other. But my wheels got stuck in the cheese!"

Pig looked at her peanut-butter-sprinkle-and-bagel sandwich. She wasn't listening to Gypsy's story. She was thinking about Cousin Parfel sailing the high seas to Bora Bora. There he was, sitting on the deck in her rocking chair, her patchwork quilt over his knees. And he was gobbling cereal from her silver cereal bowl!

"The cheese squad tried to rescue me," Gypsy was saying, "but they couldn't make it up the onions. Miles of cheese were all around me. There was a volcano on the horizon. It erupted! Waves of ketchup"—Gypsy was getting very excited—"gurgled all over the cheeseburger. Luckily I had some french fries with me."

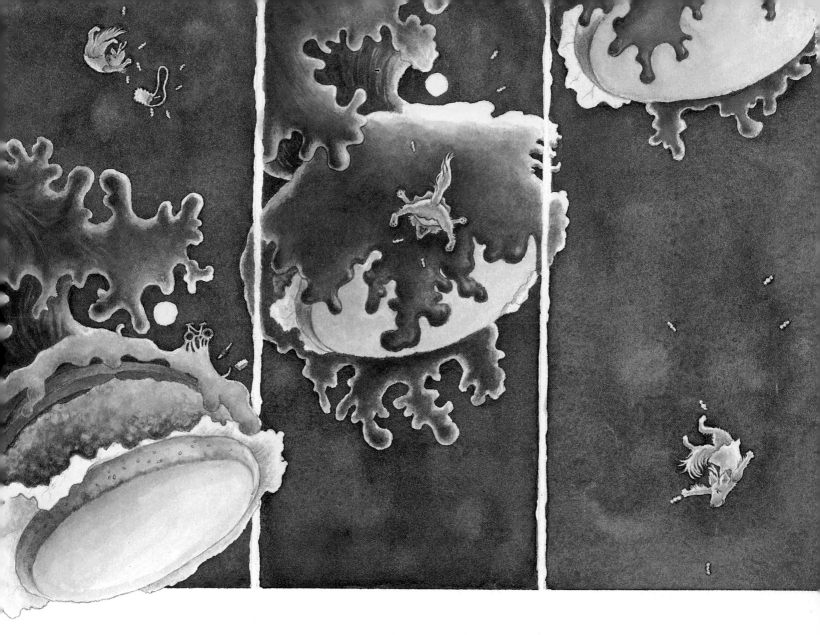

"Before you could say, I'll have a banana split—wait—make that two, I
dunked them in the ketchup, but the waves knocked me off my bicycle and
I was falling, falling into a dark space. Then I heard a voice calling to me.
It said: *'Next time have the chicken.'* Now, what could that have meant?"
Gypsy turned to Pig. "What do you think, Pig?"

But Pig was fast asleep.

"Poor Pig," thought Gypsy. "All her treasures gone. And I have so many treasures that this morning I couldn't even find my scarf. It's not fair."

Gypsy tiptoed into her house. She had a wonderful plan.

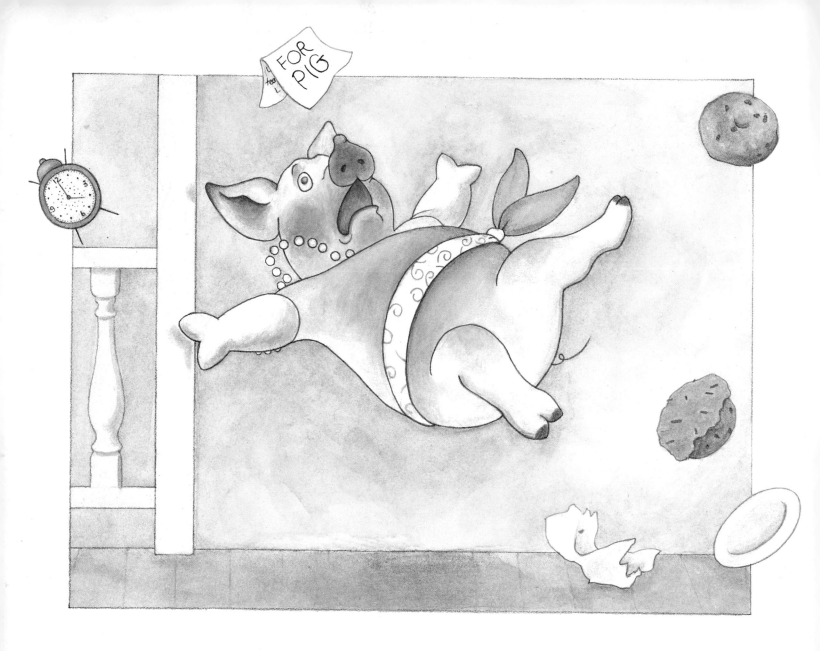

RINGGG. Gypsy's alarm clock rang. That meant it was four o'clock— teatime. Pig's eyes flew open. Beside her lay a folded piece of paper with her name on it. She opened it and read, "Dear Pig, Please come to tea at 18 Goldenhair Lane. Love, your friend Gypsy."

"But my house has no teacups," she mumbled. Pig walked to her own front door. She stopped just inside. "Where am I?" she wondered.

"Surprise," said Gypsy. She was carrying a giant hot-dog pizza. "I emptied my house and filled yours. What a cleaning day! Let's eat."

Gypsy and Pig sat in mismatched chairs and ate their fill. Pig told a story about two babies, Pig and Parfel, side by side in their high chairs. Whenever Pig wasn't looking, Parfel would steal her silver cereal bowl — but she always got it back. "It's a true story," Pig explained.

Gypsy was too tired to listen to Pig's story. She fell soundly asleep.

Pig walked very quietly into her bedroom and opened an old chest. She
pulled out an orange-and-purple paisley scarf. It had silver threads running
through it, and it was very beautiful. Someone — Pig couldn't remember
who — had left it at her house a long time ago.

Pig wrapped the scarf around Gypsy. "This is for you," she said very
softly, "because you are my friend."

The next morning Gypsy knew just where to find her paisley scarf. She put it on and went to the grocery store. Then she invited Pig over for an all-flavor ice-cream party.